Disney
FROZEN II

We'll Always Have Each Other

By John Edwards

Illustrated by the Disney Storybook Art Team

A Random House PICTUREBACK® Book

Random House New York

rhcbooks.com
ISBN 978-0-7364-4035-6
Printed in the United States of America
10 9 8 7 6 5 4 3 2 1

The seasons were changing in Arendelle. Fall had come, and Princess Anna and Olaf were looking for a pumpkin for the harvest table.

Suddenly, a **big red leaf** fell right onto Olaf's eyes, and the snowman stumbled all around the patch.

"Hey, look at that! You found us
the **_perfect pumpkin_**!" said Anna.

But when Anna lifted the pumpkin, it slipped from her hands and smashed on the ground. Olaf couldn't believe it! Their perfect pumpkin had turned into a pile of *orange mush*.

Olaf started to think about all the changes happening in Arendelle. "Does **everything** have to change?" he asked.

"Not everything," Anna said. "Some things will **always** stay the same."

Anna continued. "The *leaves* are changing color and falling all around . . .

but we know **spring**
will come again."

"The air is growing **colder** . . .

but we will keep **each other** warm."

"The **winds** are changing, but no matter what, we'll never let each other go."

"Our town will continue to grow,
but it will **forever** be our home."

"Life may get harder sometimes,
but we'll stay **strong** for each other."

"And as each day ends, the sun will set . . .
but we know it will **rise** tomorrow."

"It's true that **some** things change."

"But the **important** things never do—
like the friendship between me and you."